The Weed That Woke Christmas

The Mostly True Tale of the Toledo Christmas Weed

"From one tiny gesture, there arose such a clatter, that the Toledo Christmas Weed garnered national chatter . . ."

—Toledo Mayor, Wade Kapszukiewicz 2018

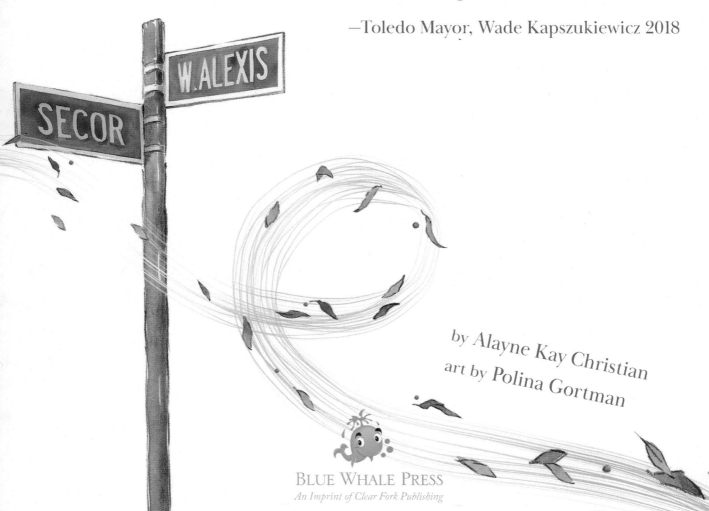

by Alayne Kay Christian

art by Polina Gortman

BLUE WHALE PRESS
An Imprint of Clear Fork Publishing

When Weed was a seed,
it *tumbled* on a breeze . . .

. . . and *snuggled* in a crack, smack–dab in the middle of a busy traffic island.

Spring rains *showered*, and Weed *sprouted*.

Summer sun *warmed.*
Weed *grew.*

Cars *zoomed.*

People *zipped* and *scurried*—

always in a hurry.

But no one *noticed* Weed.

Autumn air *chilled*.

Falling leaves *danced*.

And Weed *flourished*.

Winter winds *whipped*. Jack Frost *nipped*.
Weed *shook* and *shivered*.

So many people. So much activity. Still, no one *noticed* Weed.

One day, two women stopped right in front of Weed.

Excited to be noticed, Weed *swayed* and *waved* proudly.

But the women didn't even turn their heads.

Weed *wavered* for a moment, and then *stiffened* with determination. Someone *would* notice.

Weed *wished* and *hoped* and *dreamed* until one day . . .

A little girl *stopped.*

To Weed's surprise, she *smiled* and *removed* the plastic bag tangled in its branches.

She *wrapped* Weed in shiny garlands and sparkling tinsel.

For the first time, zooming
cars and zipping people
noticed Weed.

A man *hung* flashing lights.

A boy *spread* a tree skirt.

And a woman *placed* a star upon Weed's head.

And every day, Weed
noticed change all around.
Some people, who had
plenty, left gifts.

And other people, who didn't have quite enough, took what they needed.

Crowds *gathered*.
Camera crews *came*.

People lined up to take photos with
the famous Christmas Weed.

Car horns beeped cheerful hellos.

Excitement and *joy* *bubbled* in the neighborhood.

A man and woman passed out sandwiches and hot cocoa.

People brought more and more gifts.

Weed *wiggled* and
jiggled with *glee*
at the sights and sounds
of the Christmas jubilee.

A band played Christmas songs, street entertainers performed and people sang out,

"O Christmas Weed. O Christmas Weed. How lovely are your branches!"

Weed's branches *bobbed* with *delight.*
But not because people had finally noticed it.

Instead, people noticed
each other!

Goodness and *love* *washed* over the city.

And Weed's heart   soared.

One night, a howling chill

ROARED

through the city.

A storm *raged.*

Cold winds *whipped.*

Icy pellets *pounded* Weed's branches

Cars *crawled.*

People *slipped.*

Weed *sagged, bowed,* and *bent* until . . .

Weed was
gone.

Once the ice had melted,
all that was left was a
plain gray traffic island.

Weed's *magic* had *melted* away.

But not for long!

Weed was gone, but people remembered it!

And they remembered
the *spirit*
of *giving*.

Spring *chased* away winter's chill.
Weed's seeds *tumbled*
on balmy breezes
and *snuggled* in cracks.

Rains *showered.*
Sunshine *warmed.*
Goodness and *love*
sprouted...

. . . all through the city and **beyond.**

AUTHOR'S NOTE

This story is partly truth and partly fiction. It is based on a true story about a family in Toledo, Ohio who found an unusually tall weed in a traffic circle during Christmastime 2018. They decided to decorate the weed. Later, a woman left a gift under the weed. From there, magic happened with the spirit of giving growing more than anyone ever imagined. Stories of the Toledo Christmas Weed spread and people reported the activity in social media. It was even reported on television and in newspapers all across the United States. That's how I heard about it all the way in Texas.

Safety became a problem with so many people crowding around, and all the donations were falling into the street. So the city set up donation points near the sidewalk where it was safer. Toys, clothing, water, food, blankets, pet food, and more overflowed the donation boxes and more lined the sidewalk. The donations were given to various charities, but the gifts just kept coming. People from all over the world signed a guest book that someone had placed in the area.

Sadly, on December 28, someone stole the Christmas Weed. The news called that "someone" a Grinch. He was caught on news cameras pulling the Christmas Weed from the ground, grabbing armfuls of gifts, and throwing it all in his trunk before taking off in his car. The next day, local Girl Scouts and Cub Scouts cleaned up the area under the supervision of the police.

But Toledo's Mayor Wade Kapszukiewicz signed a proclamation celebrating the Toledo Christmas Weed and the togetherness and jollity it brought to the area. He read it on the radio for all to hear. "From one tiny gesture, there arose such a clatter, that the Toledo Christmas Weed garnered national chatter . . ." The mayor invited Toledo residents to join him in celebrating the Christmas Weed and the camaraderie and community that it inspired.

It is my hope that, just like in the story, the unity created by Weed will sprout around the world spreading and growing goodness and love . . . not only at Christmastime, but every day throughout the year.

For my loving sister Irma, thank you for always noticing me when I feel like a weed and for your kind spirit that strives to help make the world a better place.

For my soul mate, Steve, thank you for always seeing and hearing me even through the roughest weather.

— A.K.C

To my grandmother Inessa, the kindest.

Thank you for filling my sails with love!

— P.G.

The Weed That Woke Christmas: The Mostly True Tale of the Toledo Christmas Weed

Text copyright © 2020 by Alayne Kay Christian
Illustrations copyright © 2020 by Polina Gortman
All rights reserved

Published by Blue Whale Press, an imprint of Clear Fork Publishing, U.S.A.

Contact us at www.clearforkpublishing.com

Address all inquiries to:
Clear Fork Publishing, 102 South Swenson St., Stamford, TX 79553

Publisher's Cataloging-in-Publication data available upon request

Library of Congress Control Number: TBD

ISBN: 978-0-9814938-1-7 (hardcover)
ISBN: 978-0-9814938-2-4 (paperback)

First Edition

Made in the USA
Las Vegas, NV
18 October 2021